For: Maisey

Rockpool Children's Books
15 North Street
Marton
Warwickshire
CV23 9RJ
United Kingdom

First published in Great Britain by Rockpool Children's Books Ltd. 2009
Text and Illustrations copyright © Sam Walshaw 2009
Sam Walshaw has asserted the moral rights
to be identified as the author and illustrator of this book.
© Rockpool Children's Books Ltd. 2009

Printed in China

rockpool
children's books

Lulubell

Ladybird

Mrs Ladybird was having a bad day!

It was washing day, and she
had so much to do.

The baby ladybirds needed feeding, clothes needed mending and the beds needed making too!

"Don't worry mummy,"
said little Lulubell.
"Now I'm a big ladybird,
I can help. I'll go and get all
the things you need – then
you will have less to do!"

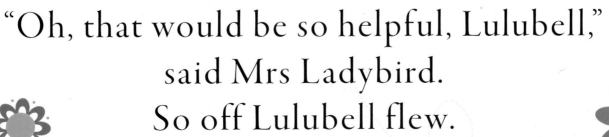

"Oh, that would be so helpful, Lulubell,"
said Mrs Ladybird.
So off Lulubell flew.

The first person
she met was
Miss Spider.
"Hmm, you look tasty!"
cooed Miss Spider.

"Please don't eat me," pleaded Lulubell.
"I need some thread. If you can spare me some
of yours, you can..." and she whispered
in Miss Spider's ear.
"That would be nice," agreed Miss Spider.

When she got to the pond,
she met Mr Frog.
"Mmm, you look tasty!"
croaked Mr Frog,
licking his lips.

"Please don't eat me," said Lulubell.
"I need some water, and if you give me
some of yours, you can..." and
she whispered in Mr Frog's ear.
"Yes please," nodded Mr Frog.

Lulubell bumped into Kitten
playing in the garden.
"Ooh, you look tasty!"
purred Kitten.

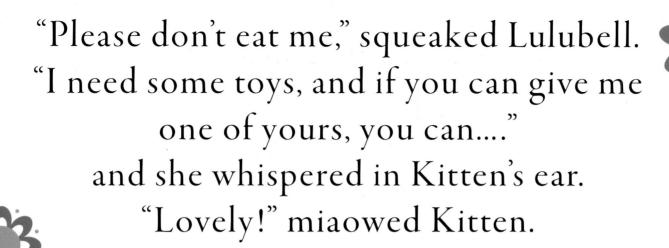

"Please don't eat me," squeaked Lulubell.
"I need some toys, and if you can give me
one of yours, you can...."
and she whispered in Kitten's ear.
"Lovely!" miaowed Kitten.

Then Lulubell met Early Bird,
who was looking for worms.
"You look tasty!"
twittered Early Bird.

"Please don't eat me," begged Lulubell.
"I need some soft feathers, and if you can
let me have some of yours, you can..." and
she whispered in Early Bird's ear.
"You're on!" trilled Early Bird.
"Phew!" breathed the worm.

Lulubell met Mr Squirrel,
who was collecting nuts.
"You look tasty!"
chattered Mr Squirrel.

"Please don't eat me!" said Lulubell.
"I need some nuts, and if you can give
me some of yours, you can..."
and she whispered in Mr Squirrel's ear.
"Perfect!" cheered Mr Squirrel.

Pleased with her
day's work, Lulubell
fluttered home.

Her tired mum was pleased to see her back,
safe and sound.

"Well done, Lulubell!"
said Mrs Ladybird.
"You have saved me so much work.
What a caring little ladybird you are!"

"No problem!" said Lulubell. "Everyone was kind and generous. I just had to promise one tiny little thing...

...I promised they could all come for tea!"

"How nice," sighed a weary Mrs Ladybird. "You really are a caring little Lulubell!"

"Goodbye!"